COUNTING

Also by Jayne Anne Phillips:

Sweethearts (Truck Press, 1976)
Black Tickets (Delacorte/Seymour Lawrence, 1979)
How Mickey Made It (Bookslinger Editions, 1981)

COUNTING

Jayne Anne Phillips

vehicle editions   New York
uitgeverij in de knipscheer b.v. haarlem

© Jayne Anne Phillips 1978

ISBN 0-931428-18-1 (paperback—Vehicle Editions)
ISBN 90-6265-131-3 (In de Knipscheer)
Some of these works have appeared in
the Cincinnati Review and Gallimaufry.

Second Printing

This book won the
St. Lawrence Award
for Fiction for 1978

COUNTING

1. HUNGRY

   He is twenty-six. His lover is an aging dancer who no longer lives in New York. She writes to him of Mexican coastal towns. She says they are bathed in a fierce light. The ocean frightens her.

In his room, a bed and one round table. Photograph of an elephant graveyard in Kenya. The animals knelt there on their knees. He has little food but he is seldom hungry. Lately, when his friends drive away, the dog whines to go with them. Not to be left alone with him.

2. LANDING

He is haunted by speckled windows of taxis. They had taken a cab home late. They were drunk and had no money. Driver's hand open beside her face. She explained a quarter was all she had, she'd thought she had more.

At four a.m. cars down the block were shells. The driver looked at her. What the hell, get out.

It was a starry night. The driver gone, he felt her near him. Blank windows of the buildings were a color he could not explain. Shadowed grey, sides of oxen. If he touched the glass panes, he felt they would move back slow beneath his hand. Old walls. Inside, the tilted rooms. And wooden stairs beaten by shoes.

3. SAMSARA

To cry is to resign yourself, she said. That's why you are bitter. You have accepted so little.

She was washing dishes in the sink. The pipes were frozen again. The toilet was backed up so they used bathrooms in restaurants or down the hall when someone was home. She had to heat water on the stove to wash her underwear. Her fingers through the wet silk seemed to waver, her smooth nails that were colored the privates of animals. Her knuckles were crossed with tiny cracks.

4. AMBERGRIS

They met at a used book store near Union Square. She was looking for Zola's *L'Assommoir*. She said it was a textbook on revenge. Her eyes were thinly lined with black. Lustrous.

She was a dancer and she trained her own company. The Zola was a prose she could imitate in form. You train them in revenge? he asked. Revenge, she said, is a way to learn desire.

He could smell a musky oil on her skin. Ambergris. The sleeves of her shirt were creased and she was thin. She wore a toy watch around her wrist on a narrow ribbon. Her pants were overlarge and khaki. He imagined her in a bathtub. Her make-up running, her eyes coming clean. Her shoulders. I supposed we were born with desires, he told her.

She laughed. We are born with nothing, she said.

5. MOSQUITOES

That first summer they sold their cars, bought a shack in Vermont. The floors slanted. They had no screens for the windows. Mosquitoes made shadows on the wall. Blood suckers, she cursed. Smears of blood on her arms. Insects squat on legs that are just one hair.

There was a hard edge to their fucking. She was immersed. She felt forgiven and she led him where she wanted to leave him. But he held her, knew how to use his hands. Knew weapons and how to use them. The third week he found a rabbit in a trap and killed it, one blow, with a hammer. Suffering, he said.

Heat storms. Dead still before the flash. An oak splintered, fell crushing the side roof. At daybreak the loud saw startled her. She watched him cutting branches, his face set hard. He worked slow, gained an angle for the teeth. Sliced the tree in lengths and split each piece. Exposed to the heart, the damp white wood had the look of flesh.

6. POOR

He consistently destroyed his manuscripts. She insisted on keeping what was left in a safety deposit box.

Her dance company had disbanded. There was no more money. They wore the same clothes for weeks, sweaters she swapped for in junk shops. Those months they ate the dollar breakfast at McCrory's. The bride dolls were feverish in their cellophane. Outside the broken drunks lined up. Her face was taut.

You're a pretty boy, she said. Why don't you hustle old men.

One of the drunks leaned blind into the window. Yellow stubbled jowls. He breathed on his hands. They saw the bloodied phlegm, the lifted eyes.

At night he almost hurt her. The Argentine couple above them never slept. Hours in the dark their chanted curses floated from the ceiling.

7. FILM

They turned out the lamps. Ate supper by the light
of the streets. Boiled potatoes, no cheese. In her hair
a sweet residue, what is left. Cigarette ashes on saucers.

When they spoke her voice splintered. He saw she was breaking
up, they said nothing. He held her feet. She rolled her
ankles, reversed at the quarter hour. She was forty-one
Her legs were veined and supple.

Late at night the old film clips reeled by. Troops of
Navarre and martial music, 1939. More refugees, claimed
the narrator. Democratic warfare from the sky, Russian
workers on parade. Is it invulnerable. Or could it be
stopped. And at Yankee Stadium it's Lou Gehrig Day, the
big man smiles. He's finished.

8. DANCERS

Smooth slap, her foot on the lacquered floor. He watched her move. In his mind he stroked her thigh. Muscled flank hard in his hand. His fear of large sexual animals, mute, expecting.

She moved at the bar, rippled her thighs. Horses. Pounding track at a county show. Blue flies bit women in hats. Children then were savage, hurt each other in the grass. Women tongued their teeth in the heat, touched his private throat.

Church women held dances for youth. Arms fleshy in yellow sleeves. Girls wore pendants of praying hands. Boys asked for partners, leaned into steps. Two women moved across the floor to show them how. When you dance, they said, close your eyes and think of God.

In the brass bar, her coiled reflection.

9. KITCHEN

    Meat is a brainy twine. Soaked in wine it tasted of sweet dark blood. Mushrooms. Their gilled caps left a moist brown stain. She saw his face, waiting, his hands on the table. Her dress was a pattern of small black hearts. Its flared skirt made her thin.

She was conscious of herself. Her pelvis arched and the egg yolks ran, congealed into a map. The kitchen steamed. She kept its wet heat in her clothes. Finally rain. The cooling food. Slick black fire escape and the soft edges of buildings.

Knowing, they were kind. Moving against some current, but indolent. In slow water. Like spaniels swimming high up, hoping the water would hold.

He wondered how much longer. Looked at the cracked ceiling. The bulb was there. She flicked a switch and light took its lines away.

10. AWAKE

She was awake, she wanted no knowledge. At night she sat by the window while he slept. She would leave him.

She watched Third Street. Charcoal shapes clung to buildings. Derelicts pissed out of windows at the Men's Social Care Center. Their urine fell three stories, clattered on the sidewalk. And the Bowery rolled like a grub, eating the dark all night.

She remembered New Orleans boys peeling their gowns. One knelt beautiful, licked his lips in a mirror. Painted them red so slow. Matrons clicking ice at the bar, small groans.

11. POSSESSIONS

She packed her possessions in four large boxes. She would leave them with him and he would stack them in a closet.

They sat on the fire escape. Watched the alley six floors down. Rows of trash cans leaned like dominoes. Tin lids glinting in the light. Surfaces dented, dappled as the scales of fish.

The radio wouldn't stay tuned. Voices meandered. Snatches of hard rock. She bit her lips. Nervous. Or her fingers. Angry, he grabbed her hands. He remembered his mother's red mouth, looking up at her as a child. Flecks of lipstick on the edges of her teeth.

If you make your fingers bleed, he said, I'm going to slap you.

She held onto him. No space between them. No declarations.

12. CAMERA

She kept a suitcase of clothes and one photograph. When she left him, he stole the photograph. He put it in a safety deposit box.

In the picture she is nineteen, backed against slick white walls of a shower. Her face surfaces in long wet hair. At first glance she is a child living someone's memory of her.

She watches the man with the camera.

He is one of her first lovers, a man past fifty whose thick curly hair she squeezes tight when they are fucking. Years later she will hear a certain recording of Edith Piaf and remember him above her; the open window, red curtains she can clench. He wants her to feel herself, push her fingers very deep. When he comes in hard from the rear she can't see what is holding her. Then he is unbending very slowly, a worm in a plant. He is amorphous, climbing what he eats. When he speaks to her they pretend he will live forever.

13. HIRED HELP

She tells her lovers she was never a child. But 1946.
That bleached piano. Ladders discolored in fields. Her
father hired help to pick the fruit. Men from the War drifted
through towns. One whose dead leg swung from a hip. Climbing,
he moved its dumb weight each rung.

At night the workers were ravenous. Over supper he watched her,
thirteen in her mother's housedress. Later he picked his teeth,
blunt nails pearled by the light of the lamp. Caught her arm
and pressed it.

He said Look here girl, this is what you are. And the bitterness
was red, with a rim.

He held out a bowl of the fresh picked cherries. Squeezed one
with his thumb. The dark pit sliced the skin. It seemed to surge.

14. HEIRS

By now she owns the farm. But she never goes back to
claim it. The house falls in, drops its boards. At night
she smells it settle.

Her father wanted boy children. Aging, her mother birthed
stillborn twins. The old man kept them in formaldehyde for
a week. Kept a light burning on wooden steps to the basement
where he kept his traps and fish hooks.

He didn't show it to just anyone, only the family and the
neighbors. He held up the jar and big tears rolled down his
face. My sons, he said. Their penises were like tiny fingers
bruised the color of bowels.

After the birth her mother locked the door against him. This
country, she always said, will fall from within.

15. AQUA

He writes letters to an address in the Yucatan. He pretends it doesn't matter where she is.

If she returns, he tells her, she will find his messages in a post office box he has rented in her name. He describes their street and says he is leaving it. Though it is nearly summer, used furs are displayed on headless mannequins outside the second-hand stores. Cuban children melt crayons in matchbook fires. They dot the cracked sidewalks with aqua. Scarlet. Tangerine.

He puts her belongings in storage. Cleans out the desk and finds a pair of pale blue stockings rolled up in a drawer. He hangs them in the bathroom and doesn't touch them again.

16. KNOTS

He is at loose ends and visits his family. They are old. Even the cousins are sixty, all of it old. They are small town aristocrats of dwindling means. The old woman in her bed leans heavily on her unbroken hip. She speaks of his father.

He would be glad you have come.

I have not come. My friends expect me in France at the end of the month.

He would be glad you have come, his son.

She fingers absently a spray of forsythia arched from a vase by the bed. It is the waxy deep yellow of butter melted to a puddle and then frozen. He feels it is violent.

17. TRAINMAN

She leaves Mexico. She thinks her sight is failing.
Each week, boys faces in the market wandered on their heads.
She takes the train to New York, she tells no one.

The morning settles its rust. Machines pour grain in Chessie
cars, shadows of a cat. A broken diesel on grass tracks is alone.
She sees its underwater bulk, a blank furred rock in waving heat.

Lengthening noon, the long tunnels. A young black woman stiffens
in sleep. Hair like a bleached fox, rolled eyes drawn oriental.
Her son stands, sways in the bald dark. Why can we get out.
When we gonna get out. His mother moans and sucks her breath.

Columned houses deserted by the tracks. In a doorway, an old
man sits in a wheelchair. Cock in his lap a limpid flower. As
they go by he waves a rumpled shirt. Flaps arms on his naked legs.
Yells Hah Hah Hah. His face burns her, she sees him cleanly.

18. CIRCLE

He wants her. He feels her disappearing. His desire comes on like acid, the air changes.

A circus camps in the town, afternoons he walks the grounds. Greased men swallow fire and bulge their black eyes. He feels those torches in their throats. The crowd cheers, tossing hats. Highschool boys in tight jeans with zippered pockets eye the trapeze girls. Lusting, afraid of their faces.

Faded straw on floors of the cages. He watches the animals. A demented lion rolls its head at the bars for hours. Rancid, stinking of meat. He sees its manged head circle, one round eye that keeps going.

How could he have had her. Not this hole in the days, its chemical taste. Her voice saying You can't get it man, I haven't got it.

19. GUNS

The old woman gives him a ring inlaid with pearl and a derringer which fits his hand like a musical instrument. She tells him his ancestor carried the gun when the land was only territory.

Back then they all died of typhus.

At night he hears bats moving air in the barn. He fires the gun to hear their gargoyle chime. Their fingered wings. The religious air smells of holes.

20. LETTERS

She keeps his letters in a box. She ties it with string and watches for the string to move. As a child she wrote herself letters, signing them Constance, Dimitri.

Tying each bundle with ribbons. Ribbons she finds in the street.

At night she sends one letter. To a name in the phone book or someone they mention in the news. Paper blank as a pebble. She uses a cheap plastic pen. She sees her hand hold it like some webbed hook. She wants to choke her wrist.

Her wrist, wound in a bracelet of lines. And the envelope is smooth and white. Cold rectangle, a piece of snow. She can feel it falling. Open this, she writes across its face, Open this.

21. BRIDGE

Some nights he drives around until the dark dispels.
Dirt roads lace the property. Cars hunched in the dark
are sexual. The hay fields smell of adolescence.

Always he drives the perimeter of the town until lights
flatten and the river comes up on his right, comes up for
years at the side of his face. The suspension bridge
shudders and the sound makes its tunnel in him. Still
the steel is buckled where one of his father's drivers
pitched into the water. Drunken, the lurching truck.

He was perhaps fourteen. The old man's face wavering in
light from the hall. Get up, we have the river to drag.
The truck hauled up broke water and streamed like something
live. Its blunt snout. He shivered on the bridge, aware
of his contracted sex, and something gave way.

22. COUNTING

   The old woman begs him to shoot it. The dog has bitten several chickens and now the young calf. They pen it up, watch the disease take hold. Spraddle-legged the hound hangs its head. Sways, rushes the mesh cage and climbs. The dog's mad eyes are marbled as a goat's, but behind the hard glass something flowers. Its rose jaws open and flare. The blooming closes and leaves him far back.

The distance is yawning, unimaginable. It is stronger than flesh or the odor of flesh, it dwarfs all things. It ticks like a clock in the mouth. It has him at the center of his breath, he is alone.

Rifle against his chest a hard arm. He begins to count.

This second edition, an international co-publication,
is 2500 copies some of which are signed.
Book designed by the author and Vehicle Editions.
Cover by Rae Berolzheimer.
Photograph of the author by Dennis Mathis.
Text face is Palatino printed on acid-free
long life book paper by Thomsen-Shore,
Michigan. This project was partially funded
by the New York State Council on the Arts.

In de Knipscheer   Vehicle Editions
P.O. Box 6107   Annabel Levitt, publisher
2001 HC Haarlem   238 Mott Street
Holland   New York City 10012

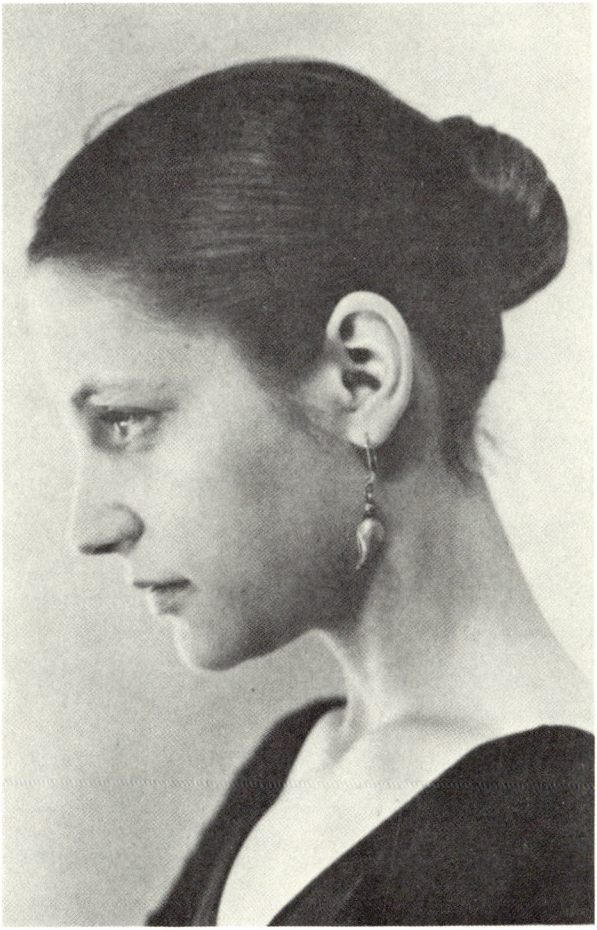